For Grandma, Gu-ma, Bat-bat, Dad, Mom, and Chris.

First published in 2022 by Page Street Kids
an imprint of
Page Street Publishing Co.
27 Congress Street, Suite 1511
Salem, MA 01970
www.pagestreetpublishing.com

Distributed by Macmillan, sales in Canada by The Canadian Manda Group

22 23 24 25 26 CCO 5 4 3 2 1
ISBN-13: 978-1-64567-556-3
ISBN-10: 1-64567-556-4

CIP data for this book is available from the Library of Congress.

This book was typeset in IM Fell English.
The illustrations were created digitally.
Cover and book design by Julia Tyler for Page Street Kids.
Edited by Kayla Tostevin for Page Street Kids.
Photo credit for pages 30-31, clockwise starting from the top left: Unknown photographer (assigned by Holland-China Trading
Company, company files held at Stadsarchief Rotterdam, digitized by www.flickr.com/people/charlesinshanghai/); Linda AuYeung;
unknown photographer; unknown photographer; and AuYeung Huen.

Printed and bound in Selangor, Malaysia.

Page Street Publishing uses only materials from suppliers who are committed to responsible and sustainable forest management.
Page Street Publishing protects our planet by donating to nonprofits like The Trustees, which focuses on local land conservation.

THE Best Kind OF MOONCAKE

Pearl AuYeung

PAGE
STREET
KIDS

Once upon a morning in Hong Kong, in the alley of Tai Yuen Street, my family was setting up for the day. We opened the store, hung the racks, checked the change, and secured the roof.

My mother promised my brothers and me a special mooncake to share at
the end of the day as a treat. It was really the only thing keeping me here.
It had a double-yolk center—the best kind!

The air filled with beeping, bickering, and bartering. Rich ladies and high and mighty Englishmen would never dare walk here! The smell of car fuel, herbal tea, and steamed cakes always wafted through the thicket of old Tai Yuen.

This is life. Every. Day, I thought.
How B O R I N G.
Nothing ever changed.

Until–THWUMP!

A thin, sweaty man with the deepest eyes and the smallest ears fell to his knees in the middle of the street.

He smelled like he had run a thousand miles.

"I'VE RUN A THOUSAND MILES!"

the man wailed as hawkers and shoppers surrounded him in curiosity.

Where did he come from?
Is he okay?
Who is this man, anyway?

He said he had **run through Forests,**
swum through rivers,
and **slept in trees** along the way.

Oh, he even **stowed away on a ship!**
He had never set foot outside his village before!
He left **everything** behind but the clothes on his back.

He **crossed the border** like crossing a finish line
but didn't stop there! **No, sir!**
He ran through mountains and seas of people. . . .

I leaned in closer to listen.

"**Bah!** We've all been there, brother,"
said one hawker. The crowd had begun
to turn away, uninterested in hearing
their own stories retold to them.

My mother called me back for lunch. And as we pulled out our bowls and teacups, the man watched us with desperate eyes.

Then we heard a gurgle.

gurgle...gurgle...gurgle!

My mother reached into her bag and handed me a mooncake—the special mooncake she was saving for my brothers and me, with the double-egg-yolk center!

THE BEST KIND!

But then she said, "Dear, bring this for the hungry man over there."

I couldn't have gone any s l o w e r .

When I handed the mooncake to the small-eared man, he snatched it and devoured the whole three-bowls-of-rice, double-yolk-center, always-share-it-okay? mooncake in ONE GULP!

Just like that. It was gone.

The man closed his eyes and patted his stomach. He took a slow, deep breath and looked around at the boring old hustle and bustle. "You're lucky, you know, kid? This is my first time being so far from my family, but it sure smells like home."

I shrugged.

But the people on Tai Yuen Street had been watching, and they slowly began to approach the man. One hawker from across our store handed him a new shirt. Another gave him a number to call for a job, and a pat on the back.

The man grinned ear to small ear and thanked us all profusely.

As I watched him go, my mother passed me my bowl.

"Ma, why are they suddenly helping him now?" I asked.
She had given me a little extra food, but it wasn't mooncake.

My mother looked at me pointedly and said, "We have to take care of each other." Then, with a faraway look in her eyes, she watched the man turn the corner and walk out of our alley. "Perhaps they remember that once upon a time, somebody helped them, too."

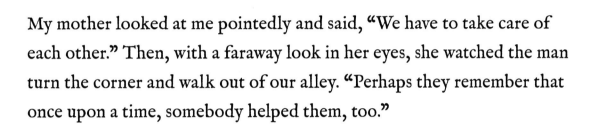

Tai Yuen Street resumed its dance of the beeping, bickering, and bartering of the afternoon rush. This was the life the man told me I was lucky to have.

I took a slow, deep breath and looked around the familiar
hustle and bustle. Maybe the smell of car fuel, herbal tea,
and sweet steamed cakes wasn't so bad.

Decades later, a mooncake shop opened right behind our store. The owner had the deepest eyes, the smallest ears, and a round, full belly. He grinned and presented a box of mooncakes.

"**For you,**" he said.

But I knew that mooncakes taste better when we share.

And so we all enjoyed pieces with double-yolk center.
THE BEST KIND!

Author's Note

This book is based on a true story about my family! And the stranger in the story really did shove a whole mooncake into his mouth.

Britain captured Hong Kong as a colony in 1842, in retaliation against China's Qing Dynasty government for not participating enough in British trade. Later, during World War II, the Japanese Imperial Army occupied Hong Kong. After the Japanese surrendered the war and the Chinese civil war had begun, Hong Kong was retaken by the British. Against the backdrop of war and occupation, Hong Kong received floods of immigrants, refugees, and settlers from the Chinese cities of Guangzhou and Shanghai, and from Vietnam, Pakistan, India, Russia, and Britain, leading to overcrowding but also a mix of cultures and people.

Hong Kong was a colony until 1997, one year before I was born. My paternal grandparents met on Tai Yuen Street by beeping, bickering, and bartering. Then they raised my aunt, uncle, and dad there. Shopkeepers, such as my grandmother, were called hawkers and had stalls that moved on wheels. I've always loved hearing stories about the wonderfully lively Tai Yuen Street's past, and I hope you've enjoyed this story, too.

Tai Yuen Street 太原街, circa 1956

My yeye 爺爺 (paternal grandfather) and mama 嫲嫲 (paternal grandmother)

My gu-ma 姑媽 (aunt), bat-bat 伯伯 (uncle), and dad, circa 1960s

My mama 嫲嫲 in Hong Kong, circa 1940s-1950s.

My yeye 爺爺 in Hong Kong, circa 1940s

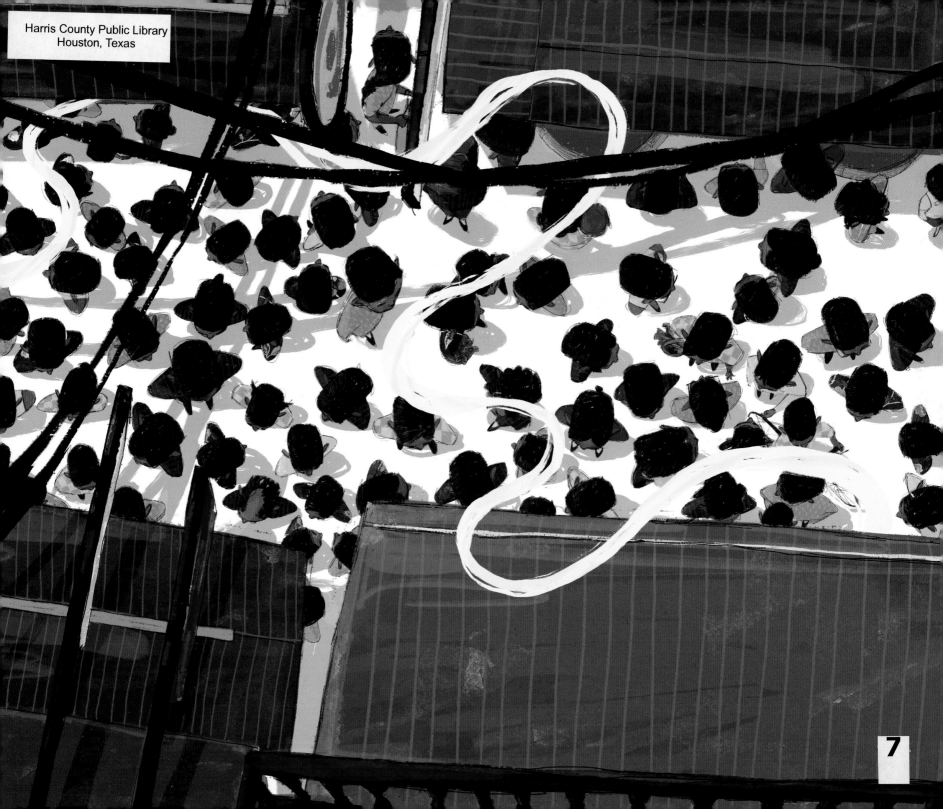